D0578292

âme
Pic BK
Vail

WITHDRAWN
UNLV LIBRARY

36961133

*H*i Diddle Diddle,

The cat and the fiddle,

The cow jumped over the moon.

Hi Diddle Diddle,

The cat and the fiddle,

The cow jumped over the moon.

*H*i Diddle Diddle,

The cat and the fiddle,

The cow jumped over the moon.

*H*i Diddle Diddle,

The cat and the fiddle...

*H*i Diddle Diddle,

The cat and the FIDDLE,

The cow jumped over the moon.

Text copyright ©1998 by Rachel Vail. Illustrations copyright © 1998 by Scott Nash.
All rights reserved. No part of this book may be reproduced or transmitted in any form or by any means, electronic or mechanical,
including photocopying, recording, or by any information storage or retrieval system, without permission in writing from the
Publisher. Orchard Books, 95 Madison Avenue, New York, NY 10016. Manufactured in the United States of America. Printed by
Barton Press, Inc. Bound by Horowitz/Rae. The text of this book is hand-lettered. The illustrations are watercolors.
Library of Congress Cataloging-in-Publication Data.   Vail, Rachel. Over the moon / by Rachel Vail ; illustrated by Scott Nash.
p.   cm. Summary: Hiram Diddle Diddle and a violin-playing cat encourage a cow to keep jumping until she makes it OVER the
moon.   ISBN 0-531-30068-4.—ISBN 0-531-33068-0 (lib. bdg.)   [1. Cows—Fiction. 2. Cats—Fiction. 3. Characters in literature—
Fiction.]   I. Nash, Scott, date, ill.   II. Title. PZ7.V19160v   1998   [E]—dc21   97-21964   10 9 8 7 6 5 4 3 2 1